Food, food, glorious food

– here comes Streaker!

Are you feeling silly enough to read more?

THE BATTLE FOR CHRISTMAS
THE BEAK SPEAKS
BEWARE! KILLER TOMATOES
CHICKEN SCHOOL
DINOSAUR POX
GIANT JIM AND THE HURRICANE
I'M TELLING YOU, THEY'RE ALIENS
THE INDOOR PIRATES
THE INDOOR PIRATES ON TREASURE ISLAND
INVASION OF THE CHRISTMAS PUDDINGS
THE KARATE PRINCESS
THE KARATE PRINCESS TO THE RESCUE
KRAZY COW SAVES THE WORLD - WELL, ALMOST
LET'S DO THE PHARAOH!
PANDEMONIUM AT SCHOOL
PIRATE PANDEMONIUM
THE SHOCKING ADVENTURES OF LIGHTNING LUCY
THERE'S A PHARAOH IN OUR BATH!
THERE'S A VIKING IN MY BED AND OTHER STORIES
TROUBLE WITH ANIMALS

Read about Streaker's adventures:
THE HUNDRED-MILE-AN-HOUR DOG
RETURN OF THE HUNDRED-MILE-AN-HOUR DOG
WANTED! THE HUNDRED-MILE-AN-HOUR DOG
LOST! THE HUNDRED-MILE-AN-HOUR DOG

Read about Nicholas's daft family:
MY DAD'S GOT AN ALLIGATOR!
MY GRANNY'S GREAT ESCAPE
MY MUM'S GOING TO EXPLODE!
MY BROTHER'S FAMOUS BOTTOM
MY BROTHER'S FAMOUS BOTTOM GETS PINCHED
MY BROTHER'S FAMOUS BOTTOM GOES CAMPING
MY BROTHER'S HOT CROSS BOTTOM

JEREMY STRONG'S LAUGH-YOUR-SOCKS-OFF
JOKE BOOK

Jeremy Strong once worked in a bakery, putting the jam into three thousand doughnuts every night. Now he puts the jam into stories instead, which he finds much more exciting. At the age of three, he fell out of a first-floor bedroom window and landed on his head. His mother says that this damaged him for the rest of his life and refuses to take any responsibility. He loves writing stories because he says it is 'the only time you alone have complete control and can make anything happen'. His ambition is to make you laugh (or at least snuffle). Jeremy Strong lives near Bath with four cats and a flying cow.

LAUGH YOUR SOCKS OFF with

Jeremy STRONG

WANTED!
The Hundred-Mile-
An-Hour Dog

Illustrated by

Rowan Clifford

PUFFIN

PUFFIN BOOKS

Published by the Penguin Group
Penguin Books Ltd, 80 Strand, London WC2R 0RL, England
Penguin Group (USA) Inc., 375 Hudson Street, New York, New York 10014, USA
Penguin Group (Canada), 90 Eglinton Avenue East, Suite 700, Toronto, Ontario, Canada M4P 2Y3
(a division of Pearson Penguin Canada Inc.)
Penguin Ireland, 25 St Stephen's Green, Dublin 2, Ireland (a division of Penguin Books Ltd)
Penguin Group (Australia), 250 Camberwell Road, Camberwell, Victoria 3124, Australia
(a division of Pearson Australia Group Pty Ltd)
Penguin Books India Pvt Ltd, 11 Community Centre, Panchsheel Park, New Delhi – 110 017, India
Penguin Group (NZ), 67 Apollo Drive, Rosedale, North Shore 0632, New Zealand
(a division of Pearson New Zealand Ltd)
Penguin Books (South Africa) (Pty) Ltd, 24 Sturdee Avenue, Rosebank,
Johannesburg 2196, South Africa

Penguin Books Ltd, Registered Offices: 80 Strand, London WC2R 0RL, England

puffinbooks.com

First published in Puffin Books 2006
This edition published 2009 for The Book People Ltd,
Hall Wood Avenue, Haydock, St Helens, WA11 9UL
1

Text copyright © Jeremy Strong, 2006
Illustrations copyright © Rowan Clifford, 2006
All rights reserved

The moral right of the author and illustrator has been asserted

Set in Baskerville
Made and printed in England by Clays Ltd, St Ives plc

British Library Cataloguing in Publication Data
A CIP catalogue record for this book is available from the British Library

ISBN: 978-0-141-32791-4

www.greenpenguin.co.uk

Penguin Books is committed to a sustainable future
for our business, our readers and our planet.
The book in your hands is made from paper
certified by the Forest Stewardship Council.

This is for Paul and Katharine Curtis, with many thanks for the food, the comfy bed, the excellent company, the hens and for simply being there.

Contents

1 Food, Glorious Food

So, there I was, lying on my front, in a rain puddle, in the middle of the High Street, with a dog standing on my back. Streaker had a roast chicken jammed in her jaws and looked immensely pleased with herself. I closed my eyes and groaned. Could this get any worse? In short – yes.

'Where did you get that chicken from?' I hissed.

She couldn't answer of course. Her mouth was full.

Besides, she didn't need to, because at that moment I saw the answer hurtling towards me – a very big man with a body built like a monster truck. Streaker took one look at the approaching human juggernaut and *fwoooosh!* She'd vanished, complete with her packed lunch. She couldn't have run faster if she'd been shot from a cannon.

'Streaker!' I yelled.

Monster-truck man skidded to a halt right next to me. He was bright red, roaring and blowing as if all his exhaust pipes had fallen off. 'Was that your dog?' he thundered.

Gulp! Time for an instant decision. Should I tell the truth or should I just pretend for a bit? I glanced at the man's bulging muscles. I looked at his swollen, angry face. I decided to pretend, otherwise I might die on the spot, and I hadn't made my funeral arrangements.

'That dog? No,' I squeaked.

'You called her. How do you know her name if she's not your dog?'

'Um – seen her before. She gets everywhere. I don't know who she belongs to, but I heard someone call her name once and I remembered it. She mugged me. She jumped me from behind and shoved me in a puddle. I'm soaking. Mum'll be mad.'

The man stared after the vanishing cloud of dust. 'Pesky dog stole my roast chicken. I'd only just bought it. Stole it right out of my bag. That was my lunch.'

'Dogs,' I grunted. 'What can you do? Nothing but bother.'

The man searched my face. 'You sure that dog isn't yours?'

'If I had a dog like that, I'd be in serious trouble,' I pointed out to him, quite pleased with myself really because this wasn't pretending at all. It was only too true.

The man's shoulders slumped forward as he calmed down, and he scratched his head. 'Straight out of my bag, a whole roast chicken

– gone. Now what am I going to do?'

'Better get another one,' I suggested.

The man raised his eyebrows and nodded. 'Suppose I better had.' He growled, took a swipe at nothing with one big boot, then trudged back up the street. 'If you see that dog again, give it a big kick from me,' he grunted by way of saying goodbye.

Give Streaker a big kick? No way! Streaker was the best dog in the whole world! It was just that she was a bit unpredictable. And uncontrollable. And a general nuisance. And a criminal and a lot more besides. Even so, you couldn't help loving her – at least I couldn't. Streaker is the cleverest dog I know, and I know, well, at least two dogs. She is probably the cleverest dog in Doggy Land.

When I got home Streaker was already there, sitting on the front step with a cheerful grin on her face, surrounded by bits of chicken carcass. Mum stuck her head out of the front window and made a stern announcement.

'She brought a roast chicken home, Trevor. Has she been stealing again?'

'She doesn't know it's stealing, Mum,' I

explained. 'She's a dog.'

'I wouldn't let her come in – not with a roast chicken. I made her sit outside. What are you going to do with her?'

Don't you love it when parents are faced with a problem and they ask you: what are YOU going to do about it? They never ask themselves, do they? If you want my opinion, parents should take on a lot more responsibility.

'Perhaps it's a phase she's going through,' I suggested. 'She never used to steal food. It only started recently. I blame it on Charlie Smugg's Alsatians.'

Charlie Smugg is the son of our local policeman, Sergeant Smugg. They have three Alsatians in their house. Three! They're always chasing Streaker and they'd been having a real go at her lately, encouraged by Charlie, of course. 'Look, there's breakfast!' he'd shout. 'Go, Hounds of Death!' You've probably gathered that

Charlie and his dad are not exactly my best friends.

Anyhow, Charlie's Alsatians got Streaker trapped behind the public loos in the park a few weeks ago. They'd already chased her way across the park and I was miles behind. There was nothing I could do to help her. I heard a lot of growling and squeaks. I was frantic. Then the Alsatians came charging back out and suddenly there was Streaker up on the roof of all places.

'Hurr hurr,' sniggered Charlie. 'That'll teach her. I hope they bit her, bit her hard.' See? That's the sort of person he is.

Streaker's coat was pretty roughed up and dirty but she seemed OK, apart from being stuck on a toilet roof and rather overexcited. But then she's nearly always overexcited, so it's difficult to tell what's normal for her really.

That's why sometimes it's hard to tell if she's being weirder than usual, but she is,

definitely. She's more loopy than ever and I reckon that encounter with the Alsatians made her brain even more lopsided than before. That's what I told Mum, anyhow.

'Maybe, but she's into the habit now. That's the third roast chicken she's had, and then there was the pizza she brought home and that poor kid's burger bun. She's turned into a hundred-mile-an-hour burger-burglar.'

That's my mum for you, always exaggerating. Even so, she had a point. Streaker had never behaved like this before. If she carried on the way she was at present, she'd end up looking more like a pig than a dog.

'You'd better do something about her, and quickly,' Mum grumbled before pulling the window shut with a bang. Typical. The dog misbehaves and I get the blame. I'm just a kid! I'm the one who's supposed to be looked after. I'm supposed to be loved and cherished, but instead of giving me more pocket money (as they should) they give me responsibility for a dog that they both know is untrainable. It's not fair.

'Taking responsibility is part of growing up,' Dad told me only last week, as we stood in the garden gazing at Streaker as she stood guard over a small mountain of stolen sausages.

'Why don't you take responsibility, Dad? You're already grown up so it should be a lot easier for you.'

Dad took a deep breath while he considered this. Then he took another one. 'Do they teach you to argue like that at school?' he said at length, and before I could answer he went on: 'Streaker is your dog. It's your job.'

'She wasn't mine to start with,' I pointed out. 'You only handed her over when she got difficult.'

Dad put a hand on my shoulder. 'Trevor, we are a family and we share

things. I am sharing my responsibility for Streaker with you, because I know how sensible you are . . .'

'You didn't say I was sensible when I broke the shed window by mistake,' I butted in.

'. . . I know how sensible you are,' Dad insisted, his voice strangely hard. 'I'm sure you can sort Streaker out, and now I have a game of golf that I need to sort out.'

'We all have our responsibilities,' I called after him as he walked off, grinning.

And that's about the size of it. I am the smallest, youngest member of our family but I am given the biggest burden of all – Streaker. Don't get me wrong, I love her to bits. The trouble is she does just as she wants and that is hardly ever what anyone else wants. She runs like she's swallowed a rocket, she doesn't know her name or what 'Stop!' means, and now she's taken to Grand Food Theft.

There was only one thing for it. I would have to go and consult Tina. In other words, more problems. I like Tina, but unfortunately she likes me too and I don't mean 'likes me' as in you *like* someone – I mean she 'likes me' as in – you know! Yuk. Thingy – the 'L' word.

I like her too and I even gave her a bracelet, but now it's like she thinks we're married or something! She always goes a bit too far.

However, Tina is smart, I'll give her that, which is one reason why I like her. As they say, great minds think alike. Tina's got a dog called Mouse. This is meant to be a joke, because Mouse is a St Bernard; you know, one of those dogs that's as big as a hippo but a lot hairier.

Tina always has good ideas and if *she* doesn't have one, she often makes *me* think of one. We make a good team. At school they call us The Two Ts. At least most of them do. Charlie Smugg calls us The Poo Pees, which he thinks is incredibly funny but then he's about as bright as a no-brain brontosaurus, so what can one expect?

Tina sat cross-legged on her bed and patted the space beside her. 'You can sit here,' she said. I stood by the window, where it was

safer, and gazed outside. 'Somewhere out there is a mad dog, hunting for food,' I murmured.

'What's got into Streaker lately?'

'Stolen food mostly,' I quipped. 'Don't ask me, but it's causing big problems. I don't know what to do.'

'Keep her locked up.'

'Tina, you are talking about the dog that has chewed through her collar and dug more tunnels under the garden fence than they had in *The Great Escape*.'

'Hmmm.' Tina looked thoughtful. 'Did you know there's a dog catcher in town?'

'What?!' I spun round.

Tina nodded. 'There's a dog warden. It was in the local paper yesterday. The police said there were too many complaints about loose dogs on the street, so the council have appointed a dog catcher to round up strays.'

'Streaker's not a stray!'

'Any dog on the loose is a stray. That's what the Dog Warden says. The stray is kept for a week and then put to sleep.'

'But we'd claim Streaker back, if she was caught.'

'The council can decide not to release the dog, if it's been declared a nuisance.'

This was a real bombshell. 'If the police were involved then it's bound to be something to do with Sergeant Smugg or Boffington-Orr,' I muttered grimly.

'Definitely. There was a

photo of B-O right beside the article.'

Chief Superintendent Boffington-Orr (usually known as B-O to me and Tina) and Sergeant Smugg had been waging a battle against Streaker ever since they first met her. It was only out of spite. Streaker hadn't done anything to hurt them. Well, not much, anyhow. OK, so she tried to eat Sergeant Smugg's head once, but that's not exactly a criminal offence, is it? It wasn't her fault he had dog food spilled all over his big, bald bonce. (It was mine!)

'But Streaker could be in real danger. We've got to do something, and fast,' I said with a dreadful feeling of impending doom. What Streaker needed was training, and training was most definitely Streaker's worst subject. Eating? Ten out of ten. Running? Eleven out of ten. But training? That would have to be less than zero.

I was astonished to see Tina beaming

happily at me. She tapped her nose. 'Fear not, little flower . . .'

'I'm not a little flower.'

'Fear not, little weed then. I have the answer you need – we hypnotize her.'

2 The Terminator

Hypnotize her – that's what Tina said.

Hypnotize a dog. As you do. I gave a rather long sigh and folded my arms across my chest.

'I love it when you do that,' smiled Tina.

'Do what?'

'Look mean and moody.'

'I am not looking mean and moody. I'm fed up.'

Tina shook her head. 'Definitely mean and moody. That scowl suits you.' I quickly shifted my expression. This was annoying. 'Now you look dark and handsome and . . . no, that's just a stupid face you're pulling. And now you look brain-dead.'

'How do you hypnotize a dog, and since when have you been an expert on dog hypnosis?'

Tina shrugged. 'I've seen programmes on television. It's simple. I bet I could do it.'

'Tina, you couldn't hypnotize a – a breadstick.'

'Trevor, I wouldn't want to hypnotize a breadstick. What on earth would be the point? I bet I could hypnotize you.'

'No way!' I cried.

'Are you scared I might succeed?'

'No!'

'You are, aren't you? You're afraid I might succeed and you'll end up in my power and I could make you do anything I want!' She waggled her fingers at me. 'Doo doo doo doo doo, look into my eyes, doo doo doo doo doo . . .'

'Tina, stop it,' I muttered, trying to stare out of the window, but I couldn't take my eyes off her. I had to watch her face, had to watch her, had to waaaaa . . .

SNAP!!

'What?'

Tina smirked. 'I just had you hypnotized for ten minutes.'

'No way!'

Tina grinned even more. I could feel myself turning red. Supposing she had? How would I know? How do you know you've been hypnotized? I forced a laugh.

'You didn't. You couldn't have. Prove it. What did I do?'

Tina fluttered her eyelashes at me. 'I couldn't possibly tell. It might embarrass you.'

'What did I do?' I yelled.

'You were very sweet,' she said. 'And charming.'

'TINA!'

'Keep your knickers on!' laughed Tina. 'I'm only winding you up.'

'I don't wear knickers,' I snapped back.

'I don't wish to know that. Now then, back to business. We hypnotize Streaker.'

'How?'

Tina frowned and stared at the floor. She stared at the wall and the ceiling. I studied them too, just in case the answer suddenly appeared in letters of flame, which, of course, it didn't.

'We need a bone,' Tina announced.

'Right,' I nodded. 'Shall I saw your leg off?'

'Ha-de-ha. I mean a bone-y bone, the sort a dog might like to eat. We dangle it in front of Streaker, we  wave it slowly from side to side, she drifts into a trance and bingo! She's hypnotized.'

'That might work,' I said slowly.

'You could sound a bit more enthusiastic.'

'No I couldn't. I think it's daft, but it's the only idea we have, so we might as well give it a whirl. I'll go on a bone hunt and then I'll bring Streaker over.'

You can never find a bone when you want one, can you? I could swear that usually when I go out I see bones everywhere. Well, maybe not *everywhere*, but you know what I mean. You do see the odd one lying about.

I've never thought about this before, but it's strange, don't you think? Where do they come from? Bones don't just get lost. They don't fall out of your body unnoticed, do they? That would be a bit worrying. You could be walking along when all the little bones in your fingers fall on to the pavement, and that would be really awful because you wouldn't even be able to pick your finger bones up, because your fingers would be too floppy to pick anything, not even your nose. Tragedy! I'm telling you, the world's a dangerous place.

Streaker was at home, keeping pace with Mum on her running machine. My Mum's a

keep-fit fanatic and she's taking part in a race soon called the Mothers' Mini Marathon. She's been doing loads of practice. Sometimes Streaker goes on the machine with her. It's one way of keeping her exercised.

'I've done five miles,' Mum puffed as she jogged nowhere.

'You haven't got very far,' I said. 'You're still in the front room.'

'Very funny.' *Pant pant.* 'What are you up to?'

'Tina and I have a cunning plan.'

'Be careful, Trevor.' *Pant pant pant.* 'You'll be married before you know it.'

'That is not funny, Mum.'

'I know. Marriage never is.' *Pant pant.* 'So what's the cunning plan?'

'Tina and I are going to train Streaker.'

SKRANNGGG-SKRRRRRRRRRRRRRRRR-FFUDDD!

Have you ever seen someone trip on a

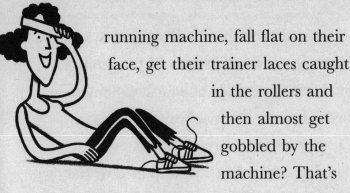

running machine, fall flat on their face, get their trainer laces caught in the rollers and then almost get gobbled by the machine? That's what happened to Mum, and the odd thing was she was laughing.

'Train Streaker? *Train* her? Again? Will you never learn?'

Huh! I put Streaker on her lead and marched off. Mum could rescue herself for all I cared. There I was, taking responsibility for the dog, just like she and Dad had told

me to, and now she was laughing at me.

I went outside and hunted for a bone. I found one eventually, quite a big one too. Maybe it came from a dinosaur. Maybe that's why they became extinct – their bones kept falling out. A tyrannosaurus wouldn't be much use with floppy legs, would it?

'That'll do nicely,' said Tina when Streaker and I got to her place. 'Look, even Mouse is interested.'

An enormous roll of shaggy carpet with a tongue at one end had just wandered into the room. He stood at my feet, gazing up at the bone, his huge tongue dribbling on to my trainers. Lovely.

I managed to get Streaker sitting on the carpet, Mouse too – a giant and a goblin – that's what they looked like. Tina found some string and tied it to the bone but as soon as she dangled it in front of the dogs they leaped on it, and Tina. She vanished beneath a

doggy volcano.
A muffled cry
escaped from
somewhere
underneath
all the fur
and legs.

'Get off! Trevor –
help!'

I waded in, trying to pull the dogs off.
Mouse stood on one of my feet. Streaker tried
to climb over my head. I lost my balance and
the next thing I knew all four of us were
rolling about. By the time I managed to crawl
clear I was covered in dog hair and scratches.
Tina lay on the floor, completely still.

'Are you all right?' I asked. She gave a weak
shake of her head.

'Need help,' she groaned. 'Think I need the
Kiss of Life.'

'No way,' I told her, leaping to my feet.

'Kiss of Death, just possibly.'

That made her sit up. 'You are so unromantic,' she complained. 'OK, just hold on to the dogs this time, will you? Ready?'

The three of us sat in front of Tina in a neat row – Mouse, then me, then Streaker. It took several goes to get Streaker sitting the right way round, but at last all was set. Tina set the bone swinging.

'Look into my eyes,' she began. 'Look into my eyes.'

'Look into my nose,' I mimicked.

She ignored me and carried on. I realized that both dogs' heads were swinging back and forth in time with the bone. It was working!

Tina sniggered. 'You're doing it too, Trevor.' I let go of the dogs and tried to hold my head still. Meanwhile the bone came to a stop and the dogs seemed to be in a trance.

'Now what?' I whispered. Tina bit her lower lip and giggled nervously. 'You don't know, do you? You've hypnotized the dogs but how are you going to get Streaker to stop stealing food? You can't tell her. She doesn't even understand her name, so how do you expect her to understand you saying she mustn't steal a four-cheese pizza with salami, tomato and mushroom topping with extra garlic?'

'Shut up, I'm thinking,' murmured Tina. She frowned at Streaker. 'Bad,' she growled, pointing at the bone. 'Baaad.'

'Oh great, that's bound to work.'

'Can you do any better?' Streaker's nose

was leaning further and further forward.
'BAAAAAAD,' Tina growled, and at that
same second Streaker's head shot forward and
seized the bone. Mouse did the same and the
next second a bone war exploded across the
room, round the room, up the walls, over the

sofa, behind the sofa and through the table,
which Mouse ended up wearing like some
strange kind of shed, until it fell off with a
loud crash.

That was when Tina's father appeared and

banished us all outside with a few well-chosen words. ('Go! Out! Now!')

'So now we know that hypnotism doesn't work,' I sighed, and we set off back to my house.

'But my hypnotism *did* work,' Tina corrected. 'I just didn't know what to do once they were under my spell. I failed on a technicality.'

'What next?' I asked.

'It's your turn,' she beamed. 'Hypnotism was my idea. Now it's your turn, so what are you going to do, Mr Brainbox?'

With a squeak of brakes a small white van pulled up next to us. On the side, in big red letters, were the words DOG

WARDEN. The driver's door opened and out climbed a small, scrawny woman with

short, spiky hair. She yanked a baseball cap on to her skull. She wore a black T-shirt, and across the front it said: 'THE TERMINATOR.' Across the back it had: 'Mission Statement: SIT UP AND BEG – OR ELSE!' Her dirty black jeans were ripped in several places and big bunches of keys jangled on her belt.

The woman skewered us with a steely glare and made her way round the van. Tina slipped her hand into mine. I would have let go, but this dog warden woman was seriously scary and I reckoned Tina needed protection.

3 Fishy Business

'Them's dogs,' snapped the Warden.

'Ten out of ten,' Tina whispered, edging
behind me.

'They your dogs?'

I nodded.

'You keep 'em on leads,' the Warden added
sharply, 'or I'll have 'em. I'll have 'em faster
than you can say "dog's dinner".'

'Dog's dinner,' said Tina. She just can't
keep her big mouth shut. She puts her foot in
it every time.

The Warden didn't like that at all. Her eyes
became thin slits and she stared at Tina very
hard, and then at me and then at Streaker
and Mouse. Some kind of activity was taking

place in her brain. You could almost hear her two brain cells calling to each other. A smile slid on to her face. It wasn't a pretty smile, more of a nasty grin. Both the dogs crept behind us and hid. So did Tina. Then me.

'Let me take a wild guess,' snarled the Dog Warden. 'What we have 'ere is Trevor an' Tina an' Streaker. Am I right? I am right, aren't I? Oh ho ho, you should see your faces. That's given you a shock, hasn't it? Oh yes, I know all about you. Been warned, I have. Been told to keep an eye on you lot, oh yes. One step out of line from any of you an' you'll be in the back of my van before you can say . . .'

'Dog's dinner?' Tina repeated.

See what I mean? Even now, when she was standing in front of Death Incorporated, she couldn't resist it. Who needs enemies when you've got Tina on your side?

'No, little Miss Smarty-Pants, before you

can say "Mrs Bittenbott", which is my name,
see, an' a name you should remember cos it
means Trouble, see? An' I'll have him too,'
she added, pointing at Mouse. 'Where did you
get him from, anyways? Elephant house at the
zoo?' The Warden burst out laughing and she
headed back to the van. As she got in she
called across to us. 'Elephant house! Ha!' She
drove off, still laughing.

I was stunned. I stood there, staring after the van. So did Tina. 'She knows our names,' I croaked.

'She knows about Streaker,' Tina muttered.

'Sergeant Smugg,' I said.

'Chief Superintendent Boffington-Orr,' Tina chimed in.

It was a while since I'd had any trouble with Sergeant Smugg and his boss, but it seemed as if they were up to their old tricks. If they'd been allowed to imprison dogs in the Tower of London and execute them, that's what Smugg and B-O would have done by now. A dog warden was the next best thing as far as they were concerned.

'Problems,' I grunted.

'Big problems,' said Tina.

'And you said "dog's dinner" to her,' I pointed out. 'That was a lot of help. You could set up a shoe shop inside your mouth, what with the number of times you've put your foot in it.'

Tina tipped her head to one side and eyed me with a little smile. 'That's what I like about you – your sense of romance. Not to mention your freckles and the way you blush when I talk about you. You've gone very red, Trevor.'

'Sunburn,' I snapped. 'Let's walk down by the lake. Hardly anybody goes there so at least Streaker will stay out of trouble – and you won't have the opportunity to put both feet in your mouth again. I thought Streaker was enough of a liability but you're just as bad.'

I call it a lake but it isn't really. It's more of a pond, overgrown with reeds and grass round the edges. Sometimes you see small kids down there trying to catch tiddlers, and sometimes there are grown-ups trying to catch whoppers. I don't see much point in fishing. All you do is stand there all day and nothing really happens and then you go home. You'd be better off buying a goldfish and putting it in a tank. Then you could stay indoors and watch it all day, sitting down.

There were a couple of anglers down there, rod in hand and hunched over the water. A rod twitched violently and one of the fishermen leaped to his feet and stared at a foaming patch of water. There was something rather familiar about him.

'It's that big 'un, Smugg!' he yelled triumphantly. 'It's the big 'un!' The fisherman was Chief Superintendent Boffington-Orr himself. I could hardly believe it. We'd only just been talking about them and there they were just metres away from us, our two deadliest enemies. I grabbed Tina and tried to pull her back, but she just stood there, gawping.

'I didn't know they went fishing,' she said. 'Poor fish.'

'Let's get out of here,' I hissed. I could feel the terrible twins of Doom and Disaster approaching fast.

Sergeant Smugg was on his feet too, staring open-mouthed as his boss heaved on the line and began to reel in a large, quivering fish. Don't ask me what it was – a haddock probably – that's the only fish I know and I've only ever seen one of those covered in batter and surrounded by chips.

The two policemen seemed pretty excited, but that was nothing compared to Streaker. You'd think she'd just been fired from a giant catapult. She almost took my arm off and I had to let go of the lead. Talk about a bolt of lightning! You couldn't even see her feet touch the ground she was moving so fast.

Boffington-Orr was swinging the fish on to the bank. I could see it all happening even before it actually did. I was living that moment

in the middle, you know what I mean? It was one of those times when you know exactly what the future holds, like when you kick a football hard, your foot misfires and the ball heads straight for a window. You know there's going to be a big smash, but there's that moment when the ball's left your foot but hasn't hit the window yet and you know it's going to and there's nothing you can do.

The fish was dangling over the bank, a
glittering and wriggling prize. The two
policemen were shouting and clapping each
other on the back and grinning from ear to
ear. They hadn't seen us yet, or Streaker.

Then she arrived. Streaker leaped like a
shark surging out from the dark depths. Way
into the air she went. Her jaws snapped shut,
but the monster fish gave a flick and Streaker

missed by a whisker and then *phwooosh!* She was gone in a black flash. The rod whipped about as the fish twitched like crazy. A moment later it slapped B-O hard across the face with its tail, twice, splip-splap. He staggered back into Sergeant Smugg. For a moment they teetered on the edge of the bank, wildly grabbing at each other as they fought to keep their balance. Then they fell.

SPLAAAASH! SPLOOOOSH!

I grabbed Tina by one arm and whirled her
round. 'Don't look back,' I hissed. 'Just walk
away quickly. Pretend nothing has happened.
Maybe they didn't see us. Maybe they didn't
recognize Streaker.' We beat a hasty retreat
and the sound of splashing and loud cries
slowly drifted out of our hearing. Presumably
the fish escaped.

'They must have seen us,' I moaned. ' What
are we going to do?'

'Don't panic,' Tina answered.

'Don't panic?' I cried, panicking like crazy.

'Keep cool,' Tina advised. 'We need to
think and you can't think properly when your
brain is turning cartwheels.' She rested her
hand on my arm for a moment and looked at
me. 'Take a deep breath. Count to eleven.'

'Eleven?'

'It's one better than ten,' she smiled, and that

made me laugh. I relaxed a teeny bit. 'Good. That's better. I'll take Mouse to my house. Streaker's probably gone home, so don't worry. We'll think of something. We always have. We're a good team, you and me – the best.'

I desperately hoped she was right, and headed for home. I found Streaker with Mum and Dad and an odd-looking man. There was no sign of the fish.

The visitor wore heavy, black-rimmed Clark Kent spectacles, although that was where the resemblance to Superman ended. His hair stood on end. It reminded me of when Dad sowed a new patch of grass in the spring. You know what grass looks like when it grows from seed and first comes up? It's dead straight and spiky. That's what this man's hair looked like, except it wasn't green. It was blond, which looked rather strange on a man of at least fifty. He saw me staring.

'Picked up the wrong, wrong, wrong packet

of hair dye,' he explained, pulling a daft face, as if to say 'Aren't I a silly-billy?' (Short answer: 'Yes, you are.') 'Was going to make it black, but it came out like this. Stupid, stupid me.'

I looked to my parents for some kind of help but Mum only raised her eyebrows while Dad shrugged. 'This is Mr Whiffle,' he said. 'He's a Dog-Behaviour Specialist. He's going to train Streaker. I don't know why we didn't think of this before.'

4 Shocking Events

Mr Whiffle unpacked his equipment, setting
up a low metal platform on folding legs. Tall
rods at the corners arched over to the
opposite corners, making the whole thing look
like a miniature cage. *All rather sinister*, I
thought.

He uncoiled
several coloured wires,
attaching them to the rods
with crocodile clips. Then
he produced a car battery
and connected the other
ends of the wires to that.
Even Mum and Dad were
looking nervous by this time.

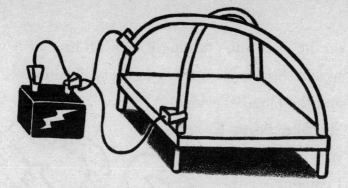

So was Streaker. She was trembling.

'You're not going to electrocute her?' I asked.

'Oh no, no, no,' declared Mr Whiffle. 'This is perfectly, perfectly harmless. There's just a tiny, tiny, tiny electrical charge. It's quite, quite safe – see?' Mr Whiffle stuck a crocodile clip on his finger and beamed at us.

I leaned forward. 'What happens if it's switched on?' I asked, turning the dial beside the battery.

ZZZZZZZZZZZZZTTTTTTT!!!

What an interesting experiment! Mr Whiffle almost hit the ceiling. He came crashing down on the platform, crushing it beneath his weight. Sparks went flying in every direction and the Dog-Behaviour Specialist began a very exciting dance. I couldn't see the exact steps because his legs were moving so fast, and he was making peculiar noises too, like a DJ sampling.

'Sw-sw-sw-sw-sw-sw-sw-sw-sw-sw-sw-switch it-it-it-it-it-it-it-it-it-it OFF!' he yelled.

Dad flicked the dial. Mr Whiffle collapsed in a chair and at that moment there was a loud hammering on the front door. My heart sank. I was pretty sure who that was going to be, and I was right.

Mum opened the door to a pair of drowned policeman in fishing gear. B-O and Sergeant Smugg launched into a volley of accusations, dripping and shouting on the doorstep, while Dad stood behind Mum, shaking his head.

'I'm afraid I can't invite you inside because you're both rather wet,' he pointed out, as if they didn't already know. 'It can't possibly have been Streaker. She's been here with us. She was about to undergo treatment from a Dog-Behaviour Specialist but Mr Whiffle is a bit, er, well, he's had a bit of a shock. He'll be all right shortly.'

Boffington-Orr ground his teeth. 'I'll swear it was your dog,' he growled.

'We don't allow swearing in our house,' said Mum. 'Not even on the doorstep. I know you think Streaker is responsible for every crime committed in this town, Chief Superintendent, but whatever it is you think she did, she didn't.'

'It was your dog,' insisted Sergeant Smugg.

'Can't have been,' Dad repeated. 'She was

here with us. Streaker has an alibi and I find her not guilty. Case dismissed. Goodbye, gentlemen.'

Oh boy, were my parents cool! Boffington-Orr pointed an angry finger at Dad but he couldn't think of anything further to say. He swung round and squelched off down the path with Sergeant Smugg, muttering grimly. As they reached the gate B-O turned back and snarled at Dad. 'You haven't heard the last of this!'

Dad waved cheerfully and whispered through gritted teeth at me. 'I don't suppose we have, not for one minute.'

By the time we got back to Mr Whiffle Mum was making the poor man a cup of coffee. I thought his hair had been spiky before but now it really was electrified. He sat bolt upright in an armchair, his spectacles hanging from one ear.

'I feel rather, rather, rather odd,' he pronounced, his head jerking several times, like a robot with a malfunction. 'What happened?'

Mum looked at him sternly. 'You were going to give Streaker an electric shock, Mr Whiffle, but you gave it to yourself instead and I'm glad you did. I dread to think what might have happened to Streaker. Does anyone know where she is?'

A good question. Where was Streaker? I hunted high and low. I called her again and again. It was habit, more than anything else. I mean, she's never responded to her name, not once, but I called anyhow, just in case. Mum says I'm an optimist and she reckons that's a good thing to be in our house.

Streaker was in my bed. She'd crept deep down beneath the covers and was huddled up right at the bottom where my feet would have been. As I lifted the duvet she looked at me accusingly with dark, soulful eyes that said: *You were going to electrocute me. Me! Your own little doggy!*

'I wasn't,' I explained, stroking
her head. 'I wasn't going to let them
do it, honest.' Streaker poked
out a long, hot, pink tongue
and licked my face. 'What are
we going to do with you,
eh? You can't go
on like this.
You've got to
stop stealing food
– and could you
stop trying to eat
my nose for a
moment? Look at
that podgy tum of yours. You'll turn into a
podgy-pie if you're not careful.'

I left her there to recover and went back
downstairs. 'Streaker's very upset,' I told
everyone. 'She says she needs trauma
counselling.'

Dad shook his head. 'No. I'm not having

any more specialists in this house. Mr Whiffle has been quite enough.' He turned to the Behaviour Specialist. 'How many dogs have you treated like this?'

'You were my first. I'd only just built the equipment. I didn't realize it would pack quite such a charge. I think I shall go back to my old job.'

'What was that?' Mum asked.

'I worked for a stuffed-toy maker. I had to stick the eyes on teddy bears and monkeys and the like, but I got bored. I'd always wanted to work with real animals.'

'I think you should find a better job than this. Why don't you try asking at the local boarding kennels, or something like that?'

Mr Whiffle looked at Mum gratefully. 'I never thought of that,' he said.

'It would be better than trying to electrocute them,' Dad added, seeing him to the door. Mr Whiffle glanced back at his crushed equipment.

'Could you pop that in the dustbin for me?'

'It'll be a pleasure.'

As he left I breathed a sigh of relief, but that proved to be a little bit too soon because Mum had one or two questions for me.

'So, Trevor,' she began, with a tight smile. 'Would you like to explain why we had two sopping wet policemen pounding on our front door?'

I told them everything. They went through the usual parent routine – rolling eyes, sighing, grunting, eyebrows going up and down, lots of frowning, etc. It was like filling in a tick sheet. Eyeball rotation? Tick. Huffing? Tick. If only they knew how they looked.

'Streaker is going to have to stop stealing food.'

'I know, Dad.'

'She's going to land herself in such big trouble.'

'I know, Mum.'

'You realize there's a dog warden out there now?'

'Yes, Dad, I know.'

'Not to mention the police.'

'Mum, I did notice.'

'They'll be watching out for her.'

'Yes, Dad.'

'So what are you going to do?' they chorused.

'Disguise her?' I suggested. That answer came from out of the blue. It was meant to be a joke, but the more I thought about it the more I reckoned it might work. Mum and Dad were looking at me as if I was mad, but then they often looked at me like that. Maybe they were right.

It had been a very long day. An awful lot had happened and most of what had happened had been awful – the Dog Warden, B-O and Smugg, Mr Whiffle – I was exhausted. When I crawled into bed Streaker was still there, although she had been brave enough to surface from the depths and curl up on my pillow.

We lay in bed and I studied her carefully. Disguise her. That's what I'd said I'd do. And how was I going to do that? Disguise her as what? Put wheels on her feet and pretend she was a push-along toy dog? Stick fake whiskers on her nose and pretend she was a cat? If only I had a cloak of invisibility. But of course I didn't. But I did have a large cardboard box full of computer games and equipment in the corner of my bedroom. Interesting.

'I have an idea,' I told Streaker. She opened her eyes and looked at me. I was sure I could see right into her brain at that moment, and her brain was asking: *It doesn't have anything to do with car batteries, does it?* I told her it didn't and gazed deeper and deeper into the black, wet whirlpools of her eyes. What *was* she thinking about? I stared in and all at once I could see exactly what she was seeing . . . sausages and sandwiches, chickens and chips, pies and pizzas and pancakes. I sighed.

'Oh, Streaker, what are we going to do with you?'

5 Boxing Clever

When I got up next morning the first thing I did was empty the cardboard box. I piled the contents in a big heap in one corner of my room. Mum was bound to make a fuss if she saw them lying about like that so I pushed the whole lot beneath my bed.

I got Streaker and put the cardboard box over her. It was a perfect fit, apart from her ears, which were a bit too tall, and her tail, which was a bit too long. However, a pair of big scissors would soon sort that problem.

NO! HOW COULD YOU THINK SUCH A THING? OF COURSE I DIDN'T CUT OFF HER EARS AND

TAIL. WHAT KIND OF MONSTER
DO YOU THINK I AM?

I cut four holes in the box. There were two
small holes on top, near the front. There was
one hole at the back, near the top edge, and
last of all I cut out a long wide letter-box
shape in the front panel. After that I slipped
the box back over Streaker.

Brilliant! She stuck her nose straight
through the letter box and peered out. I'm
sure she was grinning. I reached under the
box, found the end of her tail and stuffed it
through the hole at the back.
Then I stuck my fingers

through the two holes on top and pulled out her ears. Nobody would be able to recognize her now. Fantastic!

Streaker seemed pretty pleased too and she went racing round my room bumping into everything. That gave me another idea – I could customize the box. I got some fat felt-tip pens and drew go-faster stripes down the sides of the box. On the back, beneath the tail, I drew a small skull and crossbones and under that I wrote:

It was time to show her off to the general public. We went downstairs. At least I went downstairs; Streaker found it rather more awkward because she was still wearing the box. She kind of slid, crashed and flipped most of the way, before finishing with a spectacular cartwheel – quite impressive for a dog in a box.

I took her into the kitchen, where Dad was peeling some potatoes. He fell about laughing so much he missed the potato and managed to peel part of his thumb instead. Served him right.

Mum was on her running machine. You'd think she would have learned not to laugh and run at the same time by now, wouldn't you? You remember what happened last time? Well, Mum decided to do a repeat.

SKRANNGGG-SKRRRRRRRRRRRRRRRR-FFUDDD!

'I don't understand what's so funny,' I

muttered. 'This could save Streaker's life.' As if she agreed, Streaker gave a little 'woof' through the letter box.

'Now I've seen everything,' declared Mum as her tracksuit legs got longer and longer. The rollers were swallowing them whole and Mum was left frantically clinging on to the waistband before they were pulled right off her. I switched off the machine and put her out of her misery.

'You're mad. Both of you,' said Mum, examining the chewed ends of her tracksuit.

'I'm taking her out for a walk,' I answered with as much dignity as possible. I had to make another little hole to push the dog lead through and then we were ready for the big wide world.

I have to admit it made people stare. Some even made comments. I bumped into the twins from my class at school, Curtis and Alysha.

'What kind of dog is that?' asked Curtis.

'It's a cuboid,' Alysha said smartly. She'd always been good at maths.

'Actually, she's a boxer,' I quipped.

'Is it Streaker?'

I was a bit disappointed that Streaker had been recognized but I didn't let on. 'Yes, but don't tell anyone. She's in disguise.'

'Why?' demanded Alysha.

'Autograph hunters,' I explained.

'Right,' said Curtis. I looked at him to see if he was joking, but no, he meant it. He really thought autograph hunters were after Streaker's signature. What kind of autograph does a dog make anyway? Probably best not to even think about it.

Anyhow, my mind was soon taken off the subject when we reached the market. I'd forgotten it was market day. The street fills with all these different stalls – clothes and shoes, electrical stuff, toys, bedding, books, you name it, it's all there. And, of course, Streaker's favourite – food.

If I'd remembered, I would never have gone anywhere near the market, but it was too late. Streaker was off, with me being dragged behind. I just about managed to keep up with all her twists and turns but eventually she ran beneath a stall. There was no way I could follow and I had to let go of the lead.

Streaker continued her crazy journey around the market. I followed her progress by listening to the growing chorus of shouts and yells from the people she knocked over. Occasionally I would glimpse her, charging about like some miniature tank. The box was still there, although it was looking increasingly battered.

Mum's favourite stopping place in the market is the cheese stall. They have every possible kind of cheese there is – enormous, round, wheel-sized cheeses; big, fat, soft, gooey cheeses; cheeses shaped like volcanoes; big tubs of slippy-sloppy cheeses; and, of course, the stinky cheeses. The stinky cheeses were on a shelf all of their own and they sat there, like hibernating mini trolls covered in black and blue warts. You could almost see the smell wafting from them.

Streaker was on the cheese trail. I didn't even know she liked cheese, but she had their scent up her nose and she was homing in on that cheese stall as if she were a cruise missile with target locked.

DESTINATION: Cheeseville.

E.T.A.: Three seconds.

DETONATION CHARGE: Set for Maximum Impact.

The cheese stall didn't stand a chance. Leaving dozens of shoppers tumbling in her wake, Streaker hit the stall at approximately Mach 2. Over went the front table, spilling cheese every which way. It crashed back into the big, upright cheese cabinet behind. It wobbled. It toppled forward. Several wheel-sized cheeses went trundling away on a magical mystery tour. Tubs went spinning into the air, sending great gobbets of slippy-sloppy stuff all over the place. Several customers and stallholders were beginning to struggle to their knees, covered from head to foot in various cheese products.

Streaker, her tank disguise completely shredded by now, stepped from the box,

clamped her jaws round the biggest cheese wheel she could find and vanished almost as quickly as she'd arrived. I have to admit I was impressed. Fat she might be, but she could still outgun a Ferrari any day.

I decided I had better quietly vanish too. I knew there'd be problems. Too many people knew Streaker. Her fame was spreading, except it wasn't fame – it was notoriety. She had become a common criminal.

On the way home I passed the twins again.

Curtis was sitting on the pavement picking
bits of cottage cheese out of his hair, so I
knew Streaker had passed the same way.
Alysha seemed to have a large amount of
stinky Stilton attached to her sit-upon. I didn't
want to appear rude so I didn't ask.

'She went that way,' mumbled Alysha, a
trifle crossly I thought.

Mum wasn't impressed either when I
reached the house.

'There'll be trouble,' said Mum, quite

unnecessarily. Why do parents insist on telling you what you already know? Mum's always saying things like: 'If that fork goes in your eye it's going to hurt so much.' *Durr?!* Or how about this one from Dad: 'You've got your new trainers on.' Really? I thought I was wearing diving boots.

'Has Streaker come back?' I asked.

'Yes, and she brought half a cheese shop with her,' said Mum. 'I expect they'll come round asking for it back. They'll probably ask for Streaker too. I don't suppose they'll want to thank her for finding it for them. I reckon that dog must have a death wish. She attracts trouble like a magnet. Your poor dad's out there hosing her down. She came in stinking to high heaven.'

'It's not her fault, Mum. She doesn't know

it's wrong and she's never done anything as bad as this before. There must be some reason for it.'

Mum shook her head. 'Dogs don't need a reason to do what they do. They just, well, DO things, because they're dogs, I suppose. And something is going to have to be done about Streaker soon.'

'I will think of something. I will,' I promised.

I went to bed full of hope, trying to think of a brilliant idea, but I fell asleep without having come up with anything at all. Heaven alone knows what time it was when I woke but I do know what woke me.

There was a horrendous banging and smashing and yelling from downstairs. It sounded as if an entire army had come bursting into the house. My heart was pounding fit to burst and I knew at once that something terrible was happening.

6 Wanted!

'Spread out men! Get that blasted beast!'

I recognized the voice in an instant. It was none other than Chief Superintendent Boffington-Orr, Black Belt Tae Kwon Do and Blue Peter Badge Holder (Twice). And I knew what he was after. My blood ran cold.

At the first sound of splintering wood and raised voices Streaker came tearing into my room and zoomed beneath my covers. (What a brave dog, always ready to save her young master! Mind you, sometimes I think it's a lot better to be sensible than brave, so maybe she was doing the right thing.)

I threw back the covers and grabbed her. I tipped the rubbish from my waste-paper bin and practically rammed Streaker into it. I tied string – it was all I could find – to the bin handle and opened the window. Streaker took one look over the edge at the ground far below and immediately tried to clamber out. I pushed her back in. The noises from downstairs were getting louder and closer.

'Please, please, please, Streaker, listen to me. I'm going to lower you down. Then you can get out. Don't get out until you're safely down to the ground. Then go straight to Tina's, OK?' Streaker gazed up at me. Did she understand? I looked deep into her eyes and saw . . . pizzas and pies and pancakes.

Bang, bang, bang from downstairs, and lots more yelling, with B-O's voice booming away as he barged round the house. I could hear Mum and Dad shouting back. There was no time to lose.

I lowered the bin, praying the string wouldn't break. Down it went, with Streaker struggling, shaking the bin so badly I was sure she'd tip herself out but then, miracle of miracles, the bin touched down and Streaker was out and on her feet.

I hauled the bin back up and shouted to her. 'Go, Streaker! Go!' I shut the window, raced across the room, hurled myself back into bed and pulled the covers up to my chin. A moment later the door burst open and five policemen came tumbling in, led by Sergeant Smugg. (Might have known he'd be involved!)

'Search the kid!' yelled Smugg.

????? ! ! ! ! !

Search me? Even the four policemen looked nonplussed. I was a boy, a boy in pyjamas. Where on earth

did Smugg expect me to be hiding Streaker?
In my belly button? The cops began
ransacking the cupboards and chest of
drawers instead, pulling out my clothes and
throwing them all over the place. One of
them managed to discover my Spiderman T-
shirt, which I'd been trying to find for weeks.
That was useful. I even thanked him.

'You're welcome,' smiled the policeman.

'Dog's not here, sir!' barked one of the men. He glanced outside. 'There, in the garden! Dog in garden, sir!'

Sergeant Smugg rushed to the window. 'That's her!' he screamed, almost beside himself. 'Come on! Downstairs! Charge!'

Do you remember when Streaker went downstairs wearing her box and she went flip-flop-crash-bang-cartwheel all the way down? Well, you should have seen four policemen and Sergeant Smugg all trying to get down the stairs at the same time. That was much more fun. I thought Sergeant Smugg was going to win but one of the policemen managed to overtake him by losing his footing, crashing into the other three and sending the whole lot flying. They arrived at the bottom of the stairs in a tangled heap.

The really amazing thing about all this was that normally these things only happened when Streaker was there causing it all but, just for once, she was out in the garden, COMPLETELY INNOCENT!

Even so, I was desperate. Streaker was supposed to be at Tina's by now, not hanging round the garden. Fortunately, as soon as the police burst into the garden she took off like a rocket. Straight over the wall she went and

she was gone. Running away had always been her best subject.

Chief Superintendent Boffington-Orr leaned panting on the wall and watched her disappear into the night. Smugg joined his boss.

'We'll get her, sir,' I heard him mutter. 'Don't worry, we'll get her. And if we don't, my sister will. She's the best dog warden in the country.'

I knew it! Tina and I were right! We thought there must be a connection between Smugg and Mrs Bittenbott.

Dad stood at the patio door and surveyed the wreckage where the policemen had been trampling all over the place. 'I assume you are going to put everything back before you leave?'

B-O took a deep breath. 'My men will do that, but don't think you've got away with this. We'll get that dog of yours if it's the last thing we do. There's an order out for her arrest.'

Dad laughed. 'You can't arrest a dog!'

Sergeant Smugg pulled a newspaper from inside his jacket. It was a bit crumpled from where he'd done that very good impression of

an avalanche sliding down the stairs, but it was still readable. He smirked and handed it across to Dad.

'Early edition of the local morning paper,' he explained.

And there it was, right across the front page.

WANTED: STREAKER.

Have you seen this **dangerous criminal**?
She is wanted for **destruction** of
property and **food theft** on a **grand
scale.** If you see this dog please report
her to the **Police** or the **Dog Warden**,
AT ONCE!

SHE MUST BE CAUGHT
AND STOPPED!

By Order: Chief Superintendent Boffington-Orr
Mrs Bittenbott, Dog Warden

Boffington-Orr and Smugg swept out, leaving the rest of the police to clear up the mess they'd made. Dad sighed and asked how Streaker had got into the garden and I told him about the rubbish bin. Dad gave a tired smile.

'You'd better get back to bed, it's four o'clock in the morning and even Clever Trevor needs his sleep.'

'I told Streaker to go to Tina's,' I said, and Dad nodded.

'Right. Does she always do what you tell her?'

I looked up at Dad. I pressed both my lips between my teeth. I could feel my eyes getting wet and I had to blink hard. Dad was right. Streaker could be anywhere. She must have been so scared by all those policemen. She could be miles away, completely lost.

'Go to bed, Trev,' he repeated, putting a hand on my shoulder. 'She'll be all right. There's nothing we can do now. She's bound to go somewhere she knows. For all we know she's hiding out a couple of gardens away. One thing's for sure, she's not going far from any food that's around. We haven't seen or heard the last of her, you can be certain of that.'

I guess I must have slept a bit because I woke with a jerk. I went straight round to Tina's. It was a rather disturbing journey because every lamp-post had a WANTED: STREAKER poster stuck on to it. Imagine seeing your own dog posted as a common criminal.

Tina answered the door and the first thing she said was: 'Have you seen this morning's paper?'

The second thing she said was: 'Is your dog

fat, or what?'

And the third thing she said was: 'Streaker's playing with Mouse.' After that she let me speak for a bit and I told her about the police raid, starting with Streaker's bombing mission on the cheese stall.

'Why on earth did you hide her under a box?' Tina demanded.

'I thought it would be a good disguise. It worked too, until it fell apart due to cardboard fatigue experienced when undergoing high-speed cornering and making contact with unidentified flying objects, like shoppers. They weren't flying to start with,' I explained. 'But they were after Streaker hit them.'

'Hopeless,' muttered Tina.

'I had to do something, Tina. I've got to take Streaker out. I can't keep her stashed away somewhere like stolen jewels. She needs exercise. You've seen how fat she's getting. But if I take her out she'll get recognized, especially now that her mugshot is plastered across the newspaper and stuck on every lamp-post for miles around.'

'Really? You mean I've let my dog play with a common criminal? Oh, the shame of it!'

Tina pressed the back of her hand to her forehead and sighed. 'It's not funny. She's in deadly danger and I'll tell you something else, Mrs Bittenbott is Sergeant Smugg's sister.'

'I knew it!'

'Yeah, well, it doesn't help.'

Tina stared into space for a moment. She was thinking. 'Disguising Streaker was a good idea . . .' she began.

'I know.'

'. . . but putting a box over her was just silly.'

'Thank you, Tina,' I said rather icily. 'Thank you so much for your support and encouragement.'

'Come on, Trev, it would only draw more attention to her. What we need to do is change her actual appearance so she looks like a completely different kind of dog.'

'We can hardly wave a magic wand and turn her into a Pekinese,' I grunted.

'No,' murmured Tina, her face taking on a faraway look. 'But there must be some way we could change her appearance.'

'Plastic surgery?' I suggested. 'What do we do, give her liposuction? I guess it would make her thinner.'

Tina's nose wrinkled. 'You're disgusting.'

'So now I'm silly and also disgusting. OK, tell me, O Tina the Mighty Wonder-Brain, what's your brilliant plan?'

'Do you remember that nursery rhyme

about Mary had a little lamb . . . ?'

'Yes?'

'Well, Streaker is going to be Mary's little
lamb.'

7 Some Very Fancy Dressing

'You want Streaker to be a nursery-rhyme dog?'

Tina nodded and gave me a manic grin.
Now I'd heard everything.

'You're off your trolley,' I suggested. 'In fact
you're off this entire planet. For a start,
Mary's little lamb was white. How are you
going to make Streaker white? Paint her?
Frighten her so much her fur changes colour
overnight?'

Tina grabbed my arm and began shaking
me. 'Stop, listen, calm down, shush, just shut
up, will you, you great whingeing wombat!
Listen, there's that other nursery rhyme about
Mary, the one Mrs Travis taught us at school
as a joke. Do you remember?

Mary had a little lamb,
Its fleece was black as soot,
And everywhere that Mary went . . .'

'. . . its sooty foot it put,' I finished. 'OK, so you are thinking black lamb, not white. But how do you make Streaker look like a little lamb? She's a bloomin' fat dog as far as I can tell.'

You've got to hand it to Tina. She does have plenty of ideas, though I have to admit I was pretty rattled when she insisted I followed her into the bathroom and then she LOCKED THE DOOR! Nightmare – locked in a bathroom with a girl! Oh well, at least I had Streaker to defend me.

Tina threw open the lid of a big wicker basket and began pulling out all sorts of strange bits of clothing – a black cape with scarlet lining, a feather boa, Chinese slippers, various sparkly tops, a beard, several hats and so on.

'What's all this?' I asked.

'Dressing-up box. You've got one, haven't you?'

I shook my head. I felt rather disappointed. I'd never had a dressing-up box, but now I knew there were such things I wanted one. At least, I didn't want one now – I'm too old for that sort of thing – but suddenly I missed not ever having had one, and I was envious.

Mind you, I couldn't be envious for long because Streaker seemed to think that the feather boa was really a snake that needed to be taken into the bath and killed. By the time I managed to rescue it the bath was half full of pink feathers.

'There! I knew it was in here somewhere.' Tina was holding a black sheepskin waistcoat.

'Is it real?' I asked.

'Of course. Look, you can see the skin on the underneath. It used to be mine.'

'Yours! You were born covered in shaggy fur? Urgh, you were a monster child!'

'Ha ha. Shall we get on? Help me put Streaker's front legs through the armholes. Button it up – brilliant!'

We stood back and admired our handiwork. Streaker now looked like a, like a – well, she looked like a dog wearing a black sheepskin waistcoat and a sprinkling of pink feathers round her jaws.

'I don't think it works,' I mumbled and Tina sighed in agreement.

'It's the tail,' she pointed out. 'Her tail is too doggy.'

'Maybe that's because she's a dog.'

'Yes, probably, but suppose we put a black pompom on the end?'

This was getting more stupid by the minute. I couldn't tell if Tina was joking or not, so I gave her a little test. I picked out a pair of dark glasses with large, bright-pink frames from the dressing-up box. 'We could make her wear dark shades too.'

It was just a joke. At least *I* thought it was a joke. Tina didn't. Tina thought it was the most brilliant idea ever. She snatched the glasses from me and put them over Streaker's long nose. Then Tina really did find a black pompom. She tied it on.

'Fantastic!'

'Fantastic' was not the word I had I mind. I was thinking: *It's complete and utter bonkerdom.* Streaker now looked like some weird, four-legged, doggy rapper.

There was a loud knock on the bathroom door.

'Tina? Trevor? Why have you locked yourselves in the bathroom? What are you up to?'

'Not a lot,' answered Tina. 'Just trying out something.'

'Open up. I want to see what's going on.'

Tina obligingly opened the door and her

mum gazed into the room. She looked at the pair of us, the mess on the floor, the dead pink snake, the feathers, and most of all she looked at Streaker.

Streaker was standing in the bath in her new furry waistcoat and her lopsided pink shades, wagging her pompom tail.

'Is that . . . ? No. Is it . . . ? No. It's not, is it? Surely that isn't . . . ?'

'Streaker,' Tina finished off for her mum, and she grinned at me in triumph. 'See? Mum didn't recognize her.'

'You are going to tidy up in here, aren't you?' said Tina's mum.

'Of course.'

Tina's mum took another long look at Streaker, shook her head and went back downstairs.

'This is brilliant,' purred Tina, grinning from ear to ear. 'Let's see what Streaker thinks of herself.'

I lifted Streaker up to the mirror, even though she weighed a ton with all the weight she was putting on. Streaker lifted her head, took one look and howled.

Awhooooooooooo!

'Is that good or bad?' Tina asked, making final adjustments to Streaker's coat.

'I'm not sure. Perhaps it takes a bit of

getting used to.'

'One thing's for sure,' said Tina. 'Nobody is going to recognize her.'

'I hope you're right, because there is only one way to find out. We shall have to take her for a test run.'

'We can't go yet,' said Tina. 'We still have a problem, a big one.'

'What?'

'You.'

'Me? Why am I a problem?'

'Because you're Trevor!' giggled Tina. 'Streaker belongs to Trevor. Trevor and Streaker go together. When you go out with a dog it's always Streaker.'

We stood in the bathroom looking at each other. I had a

strange sinking feeling in the pit of my stomach. Something was up. Something awful was coming my way, but I had no idea what it was. I just knew it was coming. And then it came.

'You need a disguise too,' said Tina cheerfully.

'You are NOT going to dress me up in sparkly trousers and Chinese slippers,' I said.

'I've got a much, much better idea than that.' Why did Tina look so triumphant?

'What?'

'People expect to see Trevor with Streaker. They expect to see a boy. So the answer is dead simple. We dress you as a girl.'

Awhooooooooooooooooooo!

That was me, howling. It set Streaker off too.

'Oh no, oh no. No way, no. No. NO! Tina, I can't do that! I'll wear anything, anything but girls' clothes.'

Tina pushed me back down on the edge of the bath. 'Calm down and listen. It's simple. We're the same size. I can lend you some clothes.'

'Tina!'

'Sssh, keep your cool. Nobody will expect it. If people see a fluffy dog wearing dark glasses with two girls, they will not be thinking: *Look, there's Trevor with Streaker. Phone the cops at once.* They won't make the connection. It'll be the best disguise ever, and just think, Trevor, you will be saving Streaker's life. You'll be a hero.'

When Tina put it like that I had to admit that it all made sense. And she was right, it was almost heroic. Even so, a girl! I let out a long, long sigh. Tina fetched a neatly folded pile of clothes from her bedroom.

'Try these. They're clean and ironed.'

I studied the little pile. 'It's a skirt and top.
Haven't you got any jeans I can wear? You
wear jeans all the time.'

'Sorry,' said Tina. 'They're in the wash.'

'What? Every single pair?'

Tina nodded. I didn't believe her, but there
was nothing I could do. I felt totally trapped.
She opened the bathroom door. 'I'll leave you
and Streaker to it,' she said, giving me an
encouraging smile. Or was it a snigger?

I locked myself in and changed. I couldn't
believe what I was doing. I pulled on the skirt
and then discovered that the bright-pink top
not only had a big sparkly heart on the chest
but it was a crop top, and it showed my belly
button.

I unlocked the door. Tina peered in and her
hand flew to her mouth. Was she trying not
to laugh? I don't know. By the time she took

her hand away from her face she had
recovered and was looking astonished.

'Brilliant,' she said. 'Utterly brilliant. Now
put this on. It's my mum's.' She handed me a
long blonde wig.

'Tina!'

'You've got a boy's haircut,' she cut in
sternly. 'Put it on. Pull it round a bit, that's it.

Now, just hold still a sec.' She turned away for a moment and when she turned back she had something in her hand. I barely had time to see what it was before the flash went off.

'TINA!'

'You're my absolute hero,' said Tina seriously. 'And we are making history. Now, having gone to all this trouble, we'd better see if it works. Let's go and try it out.'

She dragged me downstairs. I stood on the

doorstep, hesitating. Streaker was holding back too. Even Mouse was on edge. Maybe they both felt as embarrassed as I did. I peered up and down the street, but nobody seemed to be staring at me, even though I felt like a Martian.

'It's going to be fine,' Tina smiled encouragingly. 'Come on.' She took my hand and pulled me down the path. I could hear a strange whimpering noise following me all the way. Then I realized I was making it myself.

'Ooooohhhhhh!'

'Think yourself into the part, and for heaven's sake, walk like a girl,' Tina whispered as we trotted down the street. 'Keep saying to yourself: "I'm a girl, I'm a girl." You have to believe in the part you're playing.'

'You're enjoying this, aren't you?' I hissed back. She giggled.

'Just remember we're doing this to save Streaker. Look, there are the twins. They're coming our way. Stay cool.'

Curtis and Alysha hurried across the road to us, staring open-mouthed at Streaker.

'Wow!' breathed Curtis. 'That is some dog! What's his name?'

Panic! We'd never thought of a name!

'Funky!' I squeaked, in what I hoped was a girly voice.

'Doo-Doo!' chimed Tina at the same time. Curtis and Alysha looked at us in bemusement.

'Funky Doo-Doo,' I said. 'Funky for short.'

The twins seemed quite happy with that, but now they were staring at me. 'Your hair's very long, isn't it?' Alysha said. 'But I like your top.'

'Thanks,' I said, blushing deeply, and inside my head was screaming: *HELP! Get me out of here!*

Tina stepped in. 'This is my friend, um, Trivia.'

'That's an unusual name,' said Alysha.

'Trivia's an unusual girl,' beamed Tina.

'Anyway, we're just taking Sssss . . . I mean Funky Doo-Doo for a walk. See you.'

We walked off. I was sure I could feel the twins staring after us, but Tina seemed happy. 'We got away with it! I told you we would. You see how easy it was?' She began to sing and dance down the pavement. 'We are the champions!'

And that was when a small white van with red lettering pulled up next to us. The side window shot down and a voice bellowed from inside.

'Hold it right there. I want words with you lot.'

It was Mrs Bittenbott, the Dog Warden.

8 Mrs Bittenbott's Revenge

The door opened and she slid out, still wearing the same T-shirt, torn jeans and jangly keys. She came round the van and stood in front of us, her mouth full of burger bun and the rest of it in her hands. I felt Streaker quiver with joy.

'Let's see. What have we here? Tina and Mouse, isn't it?'

'Bingo,' Tina smiled.

The Warden's eyes flicked down to Streaker. 'And how about these two? Just what kind of dog is that meant to be?'

'We're going to a doggy fancy-dress party,' Tina invented.

'Is that right? So what's wrong with that

black one? Why is she wearing sunglasses?'

'She's blind,' Tina answered.

'Blind?' The Terminator stepped closer.

'We're looking after her. You've heard of Guide Dogs for the Blind? We're the opposite. We're Guide People for the Blind Dog.' I trilled all this in my best tra-la-la-I'm-a-girl kind of voice. Even Tina gave me a strange look.

'What's wrong with your friend?' snarled Mrs Bittenbott.

'Sore throat,' Tina answered evenly.

'So where's your boyfriend today? And that wretched dog of his? I'll find them, you know, and then they'll be in trouble. Hiding a criminal dog is an offence. You tell him from me. Your boyfriend's in big trouble, oh yes.'

'He's not her boyfriend!' I snapped, and Tina looked daggers at me, while Mrs Bittenbott took a step back in surprise.

'Oh really? And how would you know that?'

'B-because,' I spluttered, 'Trevor's *my* boyfriend.' Aargh! What WAS I saying? Was I totally bonkers? Tina was sucking in her cheeks very hard, a sure sign that she was desperately trying to control a fit of the giggles. Streaker was sniffing the air.

The Dog Warden was examining me uncomfortably closely. 'I'm sure I've seen you somewhere before,' she began.

'That's because she lives here,' said Tina.

'Maybe. Maybe. But that interplanetary dog

of yours looks familiar too.'

'That's dogs for you,' said Tina brightly. 'Oh well, can't stand here chatting all day, we've got that party to go to. Come on, Trivia.'

Tina pulled me away and we began to walk steadily up the street. I think we would have made it if it hadn't been for the burger bun. Streaker had been eyeing it up for ages and there was no way she was going to let it get away from her now.

Mrs Bittenbott was already halfway back to her van when Streaker suddenly whirled round and took off. Her action spun me round so fast I crashed to the ground and my wig fell off. In ten mighty bounds Streaker had reached the van, now minus her sunglasses. With the eleventh bound she was in the air, just as the Dog Warden was about to cram the last piece of burger into her mouth. It never reached its destination, but Streaker did.

WHUMPP!

The bun was gone. Straight into Streaker's mouth and down her throat. As Streaker raced away Mrs Bittenbott roared out: 'STREAKER!' Then she turned towards Tina and me. 'TREVOR!' she bellowed.

That was it. I scrambled to my feet and raced off, leaving the wig behind. 'Come on!' I yelled at Tina, and all three of us made off down the street. I heard the van start up and

when I glanced back I was astonished
to see Tina running straight towards
the van!

'Tina!' I cried. She'd gone
back for her mum's
precious wig. 'Leave it!
It's only a wig!'

Then Mouse started back too! I was tearing
my hair out. This was crazy!

'Come on!' I screamed. The van had
stopped. Mrs Bittenbott was grabbing
something from the back.

Tina got the wig, turned and began racing
back towards me, only to crash straight into
Mouse. She went flying, right over Mouse,
and Mouse is a big, big dog. She
crashed to the ground with a
pained cry, rolling over
and over,
clutching
her leg. I

could see blood. Tina lay on the pavement, rocking back and forth and yelling at me.

'Run for it, Trev, run for it!'

For a second I stood there, staring up the empty street ahead of me. Escape was in my grasp. I looked back at Tina sprawled across the pavement. Mrs Bittenbott came round from behind the van, waving her dog-catching net. Was it for Mouse or for Tina or both?

'Run!' Tina yelled again and again. 'Go, go go!' She waved a hand at me.

That was it. I made up my mind. I raced back to her, grabbed her under the arms and lifted her to her feet.

'We can make it,' I hissed through gritted
teeth. 'Come on!'

'You go!'

'Not without you,' I said.

SWOOOOSH!!

The net was over us. We couldn't take
another step. The Dog Warden
jiggled the pole
backwards and
forwards, making
us stagger from
side to side. She
grinned, showing
several chipped
brown teeth. And
she crowed.
How she crowed!

'Oh ho ho, what have we here?
What strange creatures have I caught today?

I've got a little girly an' what's this peculiar monster? Is it a boy? Is it a girl? Hello little girly! Oh, my my, It's a boy! It's Trevor! Trevor the girl! Won't your friends think you're a funny one? An' look at this! Oh yes! This is my lucky day! Come on then, come on, coochy-coochy!'

It was Streaker. She had come back. She was walking slowly, belly almost on the ground she was so fat. Little wonder after that burger she'd just eaten.

'Streaker,' I said. 'Run for it!'

But of course she never does what she's told. She came closer and closer until all Mrs Bittenbott had to do was snap a lead on to her collar. She didn't even need the dog-catching net. She did the same to Mouse. Then she sat down on a garden wall and gazed at us, her face beaming. You'd have thought it was her birthday.

'I wish I had a camera. All four of you in

one fell swoop. Oh my.' She picked up her radio and began speaking into it. 'Bittenbott to Smugg, Bittenbott to Smugg – mission accomplished. I repeat, mission accomplished. I've got the whole bloomin' lot of 'em! Get yourself down here at once!'

And that was how we ended up in a cell at the police station. I couldn't bear all the crowing. Sergeant Smugg took photos of us. I had to stand in front of one of those height charts like a common criminal while he took my photo. He made me put the wig back on too. I wanted to die.

A policewoman mopped up Tina's cut leg and put a plaster over it. It was quite a big wound. It must have hurt a lot.

'You should have run for it when you could,' she said. 'Now we're all in a mess.'

'I couldn't leave you on your own,' I grunted, and Tina smiled.

'My hero,' she murmured.

'Oh, shut up.'

Of course Dad was sent for. He was rather surprised to say the least when he saw us. He wasn't expecting to find a rap-dog in a sheepskin waistcoat and with pompom tail and pink shades, so that was a bit of a shock. Then he saw me, his only son, dressed as a girl. He reeled back for a second and did a double take, like he was in a cartoon. He screwed his eyes up tight and took another long stare.

'Trevor,' he said at last, forcing a smile. 'What a constant surprise you are to me. I shall look forward to hearing the explanation for this one. I was wondering how long it would be before I had to come and get you out of jail,' he went on, almost managing a smile. 'How many times is it now altogether? Three or four?'

'Six,' I said.

'He's a liability, your son,' growled Sergeant

Smugg. 'He should be shut away with the dogs, if you ask me.'

'Fortunately, Sergeant, we are not asking,' answered Dad. 'I'm taking them home.'

'You can take them three home,' snarled Mrs Bittenbott, 'but you can't take that thieving mutt. She's a criminal and she's going straight to the dog compound.'

'Dad?'

Dad shrugged. 'There's nothing I can do,

Trevor, not yet. Let's go home and have a think about things, eh?'

I offered Tina my shoulder to lean on as she limped out. At the door I glanced back at Streaker. She gazed at me with deep, wet eyes and gave a little whimper.

'Sorry, Streaker,' I whispered, 'but we'll be back, I promise.'

Mrs Bittenbott slammed the door shut on Streaker, turned the key and flashed a brown-toothed grin at me.

'You come back as often as you like, cos that dog's not going nowhere except down the

dog compound an' then . . .'

The Dog Warden lifted a hand to her throat and slowly drew her finger right across. '. . . it's going to be doggy 'eaven for 'er!'

9 Condemned!

Sitting in the back of the car on the way home I bombarded Dad with questions, mostly the same one. 'They can't do it, Dad, can they? They can't do it. They can't just put Streaker down, can they?'

Dad's knuckles were white from gripping the steering wheel hard. He was angry, but not with me and Tina, at least not much.

'They're the police,' Dad pointed out. 'They carry out the law. They've got a piece of paper that says Streaker is a public nuisance and, let's face it, Trevor, she is. Look at all the food she's been stealing. Look at the damage she's caused.'

'I know Dad, but you can't have a dog put

down just because of that. There must be something we can do.'

'We've tried everything we can. Look at you! You've even taken to dressing up as a girl! Heaven alone knows how that was supposed to help.'

'It was a disguise and it would have worked if the wig hadn't fallen off,' Tina put in. 'Trevor was doing really well.'

'I don't wish to know that,' sighed Dad. 'I'll drop you at Tina's so you can change back. Then come straight home. I can't cope with much more of this. Your mother's nervous enough as it is, what with the Mothers' Marathon tomorrow.'

Going back into Tina's house we met her mum. She looked faintly surprised.

'Is that . . . ? It is, isn't it? Yes, I thought so. Hmm, the games you two play.' And she left it at that. At least she didn't make a song and dance about it like my mum and dad. It was such a relief to get back into my own clothes, I can tell you!

'Your mum's cool,' I told Tina.

'So's the fridge,' she answered.

'What's that supposed to mean?'

Tina shrugged. 'I don't know. I just said it because it's true. Fridges *are* cool.'

'Yeah, but you made it sound like your mum's a fridge.'

Tina gave another shrug. 'Well obviously she isn't, is she? So why are we arguing?'

'I don't know,' I stuttered, completely bewildered by now.

'Neither do I,' said Tina. We looked at each other. 'Shall we stop this conversation before it gets any more stupid?'

'Good idea. We have to rescue Streaker

from Death Row. What are we going to do?'

'Dig a tunnel?' Tina suggested.

'Normally you dig a tunnel out of prison, not into it. Besides, no time and too difficult.'

'OK. How about we steal a car, ram it through the gates of the compound and release her like that?'

'Can you drive?'

'No.'

'Nor me. Do you know how to steal a car?'

Tina shook her head.

'Nor me,' I repeated. 'Any more bright ideas?'

'It's your turn,' said Tina.

We sat there for the rest of the evening, coming up with ideas, but they were all useless. There were too many problems to overcome. We drew plans of the dog compound and made a list.

1. Get past Sergeant Smugg, Boffington-Orr and Mrs Bittenbott. (How?)

2. Get keys to compound. (Where from? Where are they kept? Don't know.)

3. Use keys or break into compound. (Battering ram? Ladder? Explosives?)

4. Get Streaker. (Ha ha ha.)

5. Get out. (Make sure Smugg, B-O and Warden are tied or locked up.)

6. Make our escape. (Will probably need

passports so that we can leave the
country. May need fast boat or light
aircraft for quick getaway.)

And when we went over our list the whole
idea of rescuing Streaker seemed more and
more impossible. I mean, where would we get
a fast boat or light aircraft from? How could
the two of us tie up three big adults?

I went home totally miserable. Mum was
pounding along on her running machine, her
chewed-up jogging bottoms flapping round
her shins.

'Don't want any more accidents,' she
panted, switching off the machine. 'I never
know what that machine's going to do when
you're around. Sorry about Streaker. Dad'll
take you to the compound first thing
tomorrow, to see if you can get her released.
I'll be in the race, so I'll catch up with you
later. You can meet me at the finishing line.'

I didn't sleep much. All I could see was Streaker's face as the door was slammed shut on her. We'd never been separated like this before. I tossed and turned and had several mini nightmares. Boffington-Orr was in one and Bittenbott was in another, which was hardly surprising. They *were* living nightmares after all.

In the morning Mum went off early for the start of the race. Dad cooked me breakfast but I didn't feel like eating much. Then we went to the dog compound. A familiar figure greeted us, and it wasn't Mrs Bittenbott.

'Isn't that Mr Whiffle, the Dog-Behaviour Specialist?' I asked Dad.

'Looks like it is. I wonder what he's doing here?'

As soon as he saw us at the gate Mr Whiffle came across. He was carrying a bucket full of dry dog food. I was busily looking around for Streaker, but I couldn't see her anywhere among all the dogs.

'Been expecting you,' he said. 'Soon as I saw, saw, saw Streaker I thought to myself: *I bet Trevor will be round here shortly, shortly.* Cleaned her up for you, too. I didn't think the black waistcoat and pompom suited her really.'

'Thanks,' I muttered.

'What are you doing here?' asked Dad.

'I took your wife's advice,' explained Mr Whiffle.

'Really? What a strange thing to do.'

'She suggested I looked for work at a dog kennel or something, and I ended up here. I like it, like it, too. I enjoy helping reunite dogs with their owners. Of course, it's sad about the ones that, you know, well, the ones like Streaker. Sad, sad, sad about the condemnation order.'

'Condemnation order?' frowned Dad.

Mr Whiffle pointed at a piece of paper pinned to a noticeboard. It was Streaker's death warrant and it was signed by Boffington-Orr and the Dog Warden. Dad angrily tore it from the board and Mr Whiffle shook his head.

'I'm afraid it won't make any difference. The Warden is a stickler for following the rules.'

At that moment I spotted Streaker. She

poked her head out of a small kennel. As soon as she saw me she came whooshing out, straight across the compound, leaped into my arms and knocked me over. Typical!

'Streaker! Look at you!'

It was almost impossible to get a proper look because she was bouncing about so much. She was all over the place, leaping, yapping, licking, jumping – she even did a couple of complete backflips!

Dad was scratching his head. 'I think she's lost a bit of weight.'

'Me too,' I agreed. I couldn't believe that a dog under sentence of death could look so happy and cheerful. Obviously she had no way of knowing.

Streaker kept nipping at my jeans and pulling at me. I thought she was playing at first but she would keep on doing it and she

kept pulling in the same direction. Then she
suddenly went zooming off to her little
kennel, did a handbrake turn and came
whizzing back. She did it three times. A
strange feeling came over me. Was she trying
to show me something?

I left Dad talking with Mr Whiffle and went
across to the kennel. Streaker grinned up at
me, gave an excited snuffle and plunged
inside. I had to get down on my hands and
knees to look in. At first I couldn't see
anything because it was so dark and besides,
Streaker was curled up, filling most of the
space inside. And then I saw.

Puppies. One, two, three puppies.
They were so small! And they
were all pushing at
Streaker's belly,
trying to find
some milk.
Cute! Fantastic!

Wonderful! I slowly got to my feet and went
across to Dad.

'Dad. You'd better take a look at this.' I
pulled him across to the kennel. He knelt
down and peered in. I watched the grin
spread across his face. Dad knelt up and
punched the air with both fists.

'Yes! Result!'

Then we called Mr Whiffle across and he
took a look. 'Aha,' said the Dog-Behaviour

Specialist. 'Now that explains everything.'

'I don't think it explains why my son was dressed as a girl yesterday,' mused Dad. 'Well, Mr Whiffle, I think we'll take Streaker home now, and the puppies.'

'Ah, now, yes, yes, well, of course, I am not allowed to let you do that and I should, of course, stop you, but, of course, I am not, not, not going to and I shall pretend I didn't see you and you will pretend that we haven't had this conversation.'

'Thank you,' I said. 'Thank you, Mr Whiffle. Come on, Dad, let's get a move on.'

Dad glanced around. All was clear. I reached in and carefully scooped up the three puppies. They were so tiny, like mice! I made a kind of deep pocket by lifting the front of my jumper and I let them curl up together in there. Dad got Streaker and we made our break for it. We had almost reached the gate to the compound when who should appear but the Dog Warden and Boffington-Orr. They stood either side of the gate, arms folded, blocking our path.

'Going somewhere?' smirked the Chief Superintendent.

10 And the Winner Is . . .

Streaker growled. She had pups to protect. In the distance a loud cheer went up. 'That'll be the Mothers' Mini Marathon starting,' said Dad. He turned to Boffington-Orr. 'You can't keep this dog here. She's got puppies to look after.'

'That is not our concern,' Boffington-Orr replied. 'Your dog has a warrant for her arrest. It's not our fault if she has puppies. She stays here. Tough cheddar.'

Mr Whiffle poked his head round from behind Dad. 'Actually, Chief Superintendent, I do remember reading in that little, little book you gave me, *Guidelines for General Admittance of Dogs to Kennels, Caring and*

Maintenance Thereof, it did say that nursing mothers with pups should be left in the care of their owners.'

'Great heavens above!' roared B-O. 'You weren't supposed to read that book. You were only supposed to *look* at it. That dog is not leaving this compound.'

'But, but, but the puppies . . .' began Mr Whiffle.

'Blast butting the puppies!' bellowed B-O. 'Get rid of them! Drown them!'

DROWN THEM!

I couldn't believe my ears. I backed off. There was no way I was going to let this happen. They'd have to drown me first. Mrs Bittenbott took several steps forward. Streaker growled even louder. And it was at that point that Superman came to our rescue. He was even wearing Clark Kent spectacles.

You've guessed – it was Mr Whiffle. Now that *was* a surprise! As Bittenbott came forward Mr Whiffle moved towards them, armed with nothing more than a big bucket of dog pellets. He tipped the whole lot over B-O and the Warden.

You are probably thinking, so what? A bucketful of dog pellets? That's not going to hurt anyone. And you're right. But maybe you've forgotten the dogs. That compound was full of them. You should have heard the racket they made!

They howled and growled and snapped and snarled. They hurled themselves at their cage doors until first one broke out, then another and another, until the whole compound seemed to be squirming with dogs hungry for pellets.

Down went B-O. Down went the Warden. They weren't being harmed – just sort of licked to death. The more they rolled about

the more pellets they picked up on their clothes, and the more pellets they picked up the madder the dogs went. Dad and I slipped out of the compound and left them to it.

'I'd better come with you,' said Mr Whiffle a trifle sadly. 'I think I've probably just lost my job, and I only started yesterday. I was quite, quite, quite enjoying it.'

'You're better off not working for those two madmen,' muttered Dad. 'Come on, into the car.'

Dad had barely got the car started when a dog went zooming past us, quickly followed by another, and then several more. I looked back. They were streaming out of the compound, every one of them. Streaker hung her head over the open window and watched with

growing excitement as the dogs streamed past. She couldn't stand it any longer. She just had to join in. With one leap she was out, spilling on to the road, her legs already churning like helicopter rotors, and she was off.

'Streaker!' I yelled. It's that old habit. I can't break it.

But she was running with the pack, leapfrogging, or rather leap-dogging her way to the front and there was no stopping her.

Boffington-Orr and Bittenbott had struggled to their feet, shouting and waving their arms ferociously.

'Uh-oh,' said Dad, gazing at them in his

rear-view mirror. 'Trouble. Better get a move on.' He put his foot on the gas and we took off.

'Where are we going?' I asked.

'We promised your mother we'd be at the finishing line. She's been practising and practising. We've got to be there, Trevor. The pups can come too.'

'What about Streaker?'

Dad gave a little frown. 'She'll turn up. She always does, not necessarily when you want her to, of course, but she does turn up. Eventually.'

'Can we pick Tina up on the way? Please?'

Dad reckoned we had just about enough time. I was dying to show her the pups and tell her about the great escape. I knew she'd be overwhelmed, and she was.

'They are so cute! Give them to me. I want to cuddle them. Gimme, gimme!'

Dad found somewhere to park and we

made our way towards the finishing line for the race. I still had the pups curled up in my jumper. We managed to push our way to the front.

'Can't see anyone yet,' I said, peering down the empty road.

'They could be ages,' murmured Dad, craning his neck.

'I was a champion,' Mr Whiffle offered, rather unexpectedly. He didn't look very sporty.

'Really? It wasn't for electrocuting things, was it?' asked Dad.

'No, no, no! Don't be silly. I was Bogman 2005.'

I almost dropped the puppies and Dad choked for a second. 'I beg your pardon?' he spluttered.

'I was Bogman. I did bog-snorkelling.'

Bog-snorkelling? It sounded like the most gruesomely gruesome hobby I'd ever heard of.

'Yes,' nodded Mr Whiffle. 'You wear a wetsuit, diving mask and snorkel, and you jump, you jump into a ditch full of sloppy, sloppy mud and peat and weed and so on and off you go. It's quite good for someone like me, with short sight. It's so filthy, filthy, filthy in that water you can't see where you're going, so being short-sighted is no disadvantage at all. I won the local championship – Bogman 2005.'

So Mr Whiffle really was a kind of superhero! Bogman! Don't people do weird things?

An excited roar from the crowd quickly changed to guffaws of laughter as the front

runners came into the view. And the front
runners were . . . dogs. Dogs, dogs and more
dogs, and right at the front was – yes, of
course, who else? Streaker!

Streaker was loping along, at least fifty
metres ahead of the rest. She wasn't even
going at
full speed.
She'd set her
legs to super-cruise
and was loping along,
enjoying the sunshine, the
freedom and the crowds
yelling. And for once the crowds weren't
chasing after her. They weren't yelling at her
to stop. They were shouting encouragement! I
could see Curtis and Alysha on the opposite
side. They were shouting too.

We all were.

'Go, Streaker, go!'

Everyone thought it was fantastic. Then the

human runners came round the corner and into sight, a great mass of them. I searched for Mum.

'There she is!' I cried, jumping up and down so much that the pups protested with little squeaks and I hurriedly calmed down.

We cheered until we were hoarse. The dogs went piling past us. Streaker skidded to a halt just before the tape. She sat down and began to wash herself. Oh no!

'Streaker!' I yelled, so she ignored me as usual and carried on licking herself. The other dogs were catching up. Streaker got to her feet and scratched herself behind the ears. She stretched. She yawned. She had a widdle in the middle of the road.

And then, and then she calmly stepped over the line. She sat up and grinned at the cheering crowd, saw me, came steaming over at a hundred miles an hour, threw herself into the air and landed among the puppies.

'Hooray!' screamed the crowd, and Mr Whiffle's spectacles fell off from jumping about too much. Tina threw her arms round me and kissed my cheek.

'I saw that,' said Dad. 'I warned you, Trevor. It's one long slippery slope from now on.'

Tina gave Dad a rather sharp look, smiled, reached up and pecked his cheek too. You should have seen Dad's face. Talk about red! One of the runners yelled out, 'I saw that, Tina! You've already got a boyfriend. Leave my husband alone!'

It was Mum. She'd come third! Amazing. My mum – third! (And thanks for

embarrassing me in front of all those people, Mum.) The slower runners began to toil past, puffing and panting until it seemed that there was nobody left.

But there was. Round that final corner came the two last runners: Chief Superintendent Boffington-Orr and Mrs Bittenbott. A quiet cheer went up from the crowd, along with a ripple of laughter. B-O waved a fist.

'Stop that dog,' he croaked, his voice hoarse from too much shouting.

'Which one?' Dad laughed. 'There must have been at least fifty of them!'

Mrs Bittenbott could barely stand. 'I'll get that dog before you can say . . .'

'Dog's dinner?' suggested Tina, and the Dog Warden sank to her knees and gave up. The Terminator had just been terminated.

And that was about it. Mum got a medal for being third in the Mothers' Marathon. Streaker got a special medal for being fastest dog-mother, even though dogs hadn't meant to be in the race at all. She also got a reprieve. The town council said it was obvious that Streaker was stealing food because she had her pups to feed.

I didn't bother to point out that we fed her very well and she was just being greedy really. I thought it better to keep quiet. Sometimes it's better to keep quiet, isn't it?

There are four Streakers in our house now. One big one and three very small ones.

'They're gorgeous,' sighed Tina. 'I wonder who the dad was?'

'They look as if they've got a lot of Alsatian in them,' Mum suggested. My eyes almost popped out. Alsatian? Tina and I stared at each other in horror. That would mean . . . no, surely not, not one of Charlie Smugg's dogs! If one of his Alsatians was the father, that would make Charlie Smugg almost like the puppies' uncle or something! Uncle Charlie! Nooooooo!

Dad fixed a beady eye on the three little wrigglers. 'They are definitely going to be trained,' he informed everyone.

'That should prove interesting to watch,'

Tina whispered in my ear.

'They are going to know their names,' declared Dad. 'They will know what "sit" and "stay" and "come back" all mean. Won't they, Trevor?'

I looked at him. Surely he wasn't expecting me to take responsibility for them?

'What *are* their names?' I asked.

'Don't know,' said Dad.

'No idea,' said Mum.

So that's something to think about. Tina and I took Streaker and the pups up to my room, where they curled up on the bed.

'We'll have to think of good names,' said Tina. 'Something that fits their character.'

I knelt on the floor by the bed and looked at them carefully. Something that suited their character. I gazed into their eyes. What could I see? Pies, pizzas and pancakes. Pancakes, pizzas and pies.

Oh dear.

Trouble ahead.